The Dolphin King

A folk tale from France

Written by Saviour Pirotta
Illustrated by Fausto Bianchi

Collins

Jean and his friends were fishermen.

Jean said, "I can throw a spear
better than any of you."
He hurled his spear at a dolphin.

The animal screamed and dived
beneath the waves.

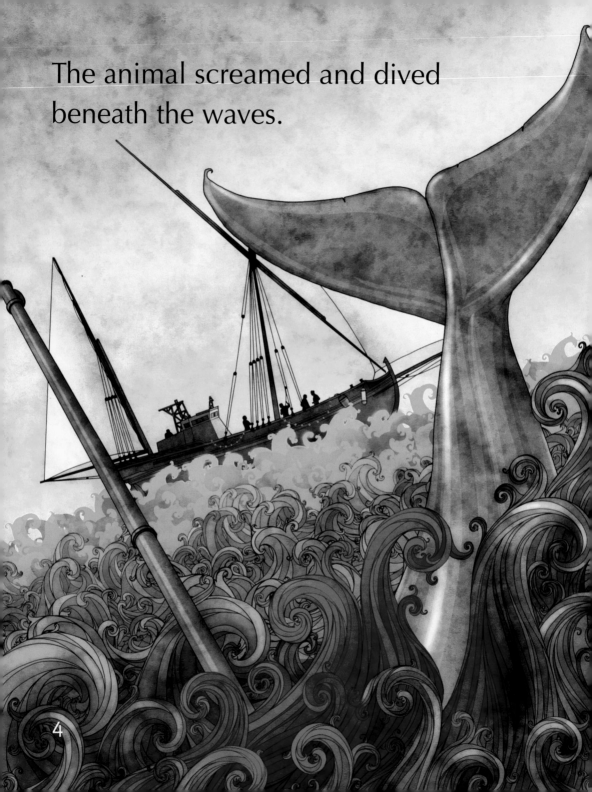

Suddenly, a fierce storm blew up and it looked as though the boat might sink.

Then Jean and his friends saw
a strange knight rising out of
the waves.

The knight shouted, "You nearly killed the dolphin king, and for this, you'll all drown!"

Jean cried, "No, I alone threw the spear. Take me."

The knight carried Jean down
to the bottom of the sea.

There, the dolphin king was waiting.
The knight whispered to Jean,
"You must heal him."

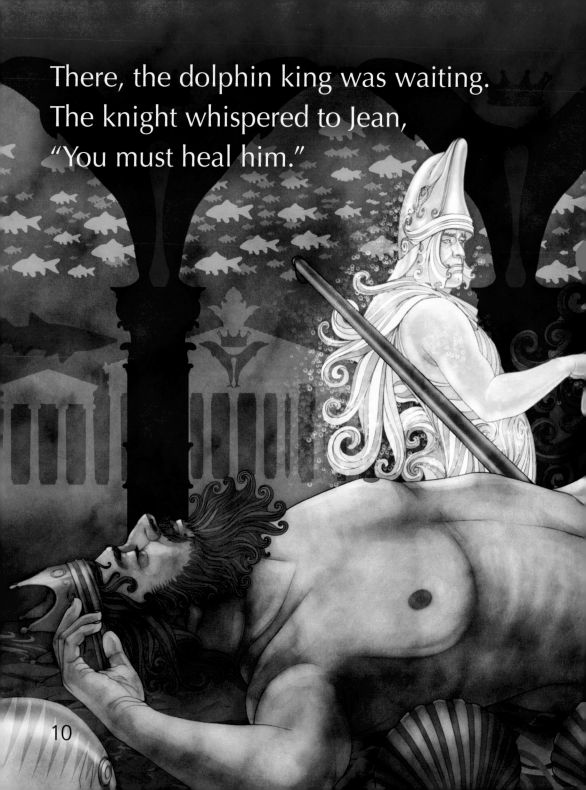

Gently, Jean removed the spear.
He cleaned the wound.
The king opened his eyes and said,
"Promise me that you and your friends
will never hunt dolphins again."
Jean cried, "I promise."

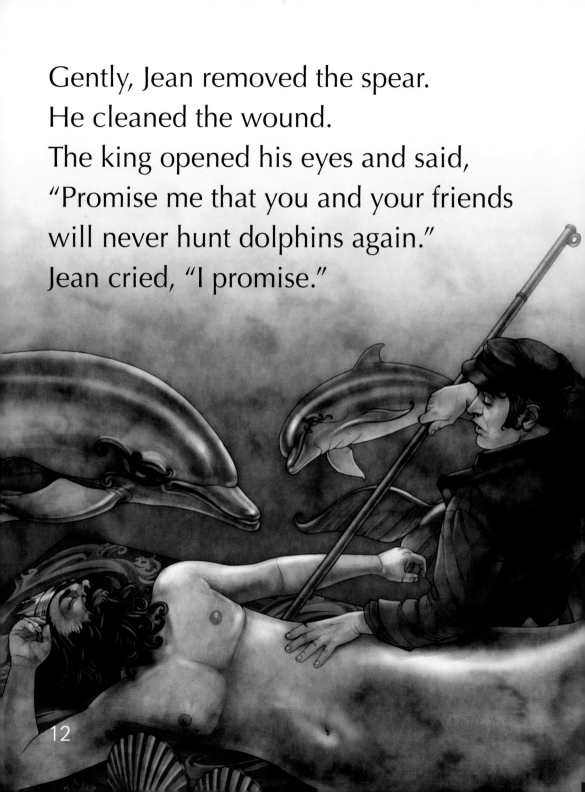

The knight took him back to
the boat. The storm had died and
Jean's friends were saved.

Before Jean threw the spear

After Jean threw the spear

Ideas for reading

Written by Gillian Howell
Primary Literacy Consultant

Learning objectives: *(reading objectives correspond with Blue band; all other objectives correspond with Copper band)* use phonics to read unknown or difficult words; infer characters' feelings in fiction; empathise with characters and debate moral dilemmas portrayed in texts; choose and prepare stories for performance, identifying appropriate expression, tone, volume and use of voices and other sounds; select and use a range of technical and descriptive vocabulary; use beginning, middle and end to write narratives in which events are sequenced logically and conflicts resolved

Curriculum links: Citizenship: Animals and us

High frequency words: from, his, were, will, be, than, as, out, take, down, there, must, him, that, your, again, took, back, had

Interest words: dolphin, spear, hurled, screamed, dived, beneath, fierce, knight, shouted, brought, whispered, removed, wound

Resources: paper, pens, collage materials

Word count: 172

Getting started

- Look at the cover and read the title. Ask the children what they know about dolphins, such as where they live. Have any of them seen dolphins, either in the wild or in captivity?

- Explain that this story is a retelling of a legend from another culture. Talk about other legends the children have read. Ask them to describe the sort of characters and morals that feature in legends.

- Read the back cover blurb and look through the illustrations. Ask the children to predict what they think the story will be about and explain why.

Reading and responding

- Ask the children to read the story together. On p3, point out the word *spear* and ask the children to break it into phonemes. Check they understand what a spear is.

- Pause at significant events, e.g. p5. Ask them if they think the sudden storm is significant in the story. What do they think caused the storm?

- When the children have read pp6–7, point out the silent *k* in the word *knight* and ask the children if they can think of other words with a silent *k*, e.g. know. Ask where they think the knight came from and why.